For my very own Charlie Bear

Love Mummy
x

My Little
Bear
Books

First Published 2013

Charlie Bear
Won't Go to Sleep

Written by Hayley Mitchell   Illustrated by Sarah Roberts

Charlie Bear was crying,

 Charlie Bear was sad.

Charlie Bear's wailing,

Was driving his mother mad!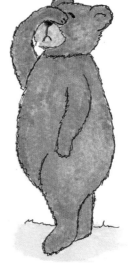

She tried to sing him lullabies and rock him to and fro,

But Charlie Bear was stubborn and to sleep he would not go.

So Mummy Bear feeling quite perplexed, went to ask a sheep,

'Oh Ba Ba can't you see I'm vexed? How can I make him sleep?'

'Well have you tried counting sheep as they jump a wooden gate?'

Mummy Bear said, 'I'll try it now, if it works it will be great.'

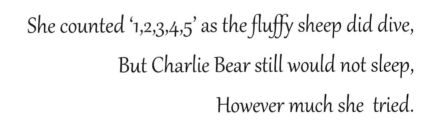

She counted '1,2,3,4,5' as the fluffy sheep did dive,

But Charlie Bear still would not sleep,

However much she tried.

So Mummy Bear still feeling glum, sought advice from Hungry Lion,

'Please, oh please, oh Lion, oh chum, how can I stop him crying?'

Lion sneered and picked his teeth,
saying in a lazy roar,
'Just let the young cub cry it out
and soon he'll surely snore.'

She tried to let her bear cub sob,

But it was more than she could bare,

'If Charlie won't stop crying soon,

I'll pull out all my hair!'

Next Mummy Bear in a dreadful state, went to ask the fat, white geese.

She stood amongst her feathered friends and begged, 'Give me a little peace.'

The geese replied in unison,

with a noisy

HISS

'Try patting him on the back,

As you give him a little kiss.'

She patted him just like they said,

But didn't have any luck.

Now starting to lose her temper she sulked,

'I should have asked the duck!'

Poor Mummy Bear was miserable and feeling quite low and doleful.

She sought the help of Badger, as her situation had turned woeful.

Badger burrowed in his den and

returned with a handful of grubs.

'Try feeding the young whippersnapper,

these are perfect for little cubs.'

But each time she put a paw full in, Charlie Bear would start to shout,

And after trying for ten whole minutes, each grub had fallen out!

The sound of Charlie's crying had risen to a yelp.

So Mummy Bear sought out Fox and asked her for some help.

'What am I to do when he cries so much he just won't stop?'

'Try bouncing him up and down, as you jump and skip and hop.'

So Mummy Bear did jig and dance and dance and jig and bounce,

But Charlie Bear would not stop and continued to scream and flounce.

Wandering sadly by the pond,
she'd started to lose all hope.
She saw Frog with his family and asked,
'How do you froggies cope?'

'Try wrapping him up in a lily pad, littleuns like to feel safe and snug.'

And with that he dived into the pond, followed by his froglets,

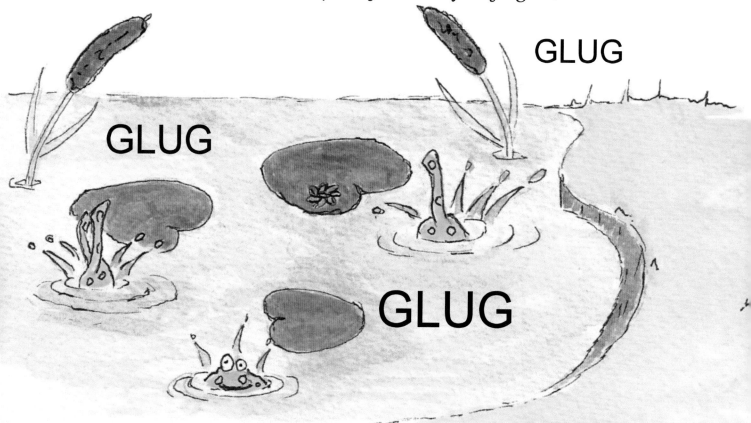

GLUG

GLUG

GLUG

So Mummy Bear, did indeed wrap Charlie nice and tight,

But the crying only worsened, as sleep he tried to fight.

The sky began to darken, as did Mummy Bear's mood.

So she questioned Mother Hen on how she kept her happy brood.

'Try laying him on his tummy, place him nice and flat,

I often tell new mummy hens that their babies will like that.'

So she laid him on his belly,

On the soft and mossy ground,

But still he would not sleep,

No answer could be found.

As she looked up to the sky, she saw the birds above,
'Help me with this problem please, oh beautiful white dove.'

'My babies like to fly up high and **SWOOSH** gently through the air,

Perhaps you could try a similar thing with little Charlie Bear?'

So she raised him in the sky, and flew him like a plane...

But the crying didn't cease and her efforts were in vain.

She came across some
tall trees and amongst
them a giraffe,
'I don't know how you do it,
how do you make
them laugh?'
'My baby likes a tickle,
with a feather on his toes.'
She plucked a feather from
a nest and said,
'Here, try one of those.'

Mummy Bear tickled him, from his feet right to his nose,

But all the tickling in the world would not ease poor Charlie's woes.

She went to see wise old Owl, who was bound to have a plan.

'The only thing to be done my dear, is love him as only you can.'

And so Mummy Bear held him close and whispered in his ear,

'I love you so much Charlie Bear, sweet dreams my little dear'

And slowly his eyes started to droop and she heard a little snore,

For Charlie Bear had drifted off and was awake no more.

Charlie Bear was sleeping,

finally at rest,

And Mummy Bear smiled

and thought,

'I like him awake the best!'

Join Charlie in a new adventure...

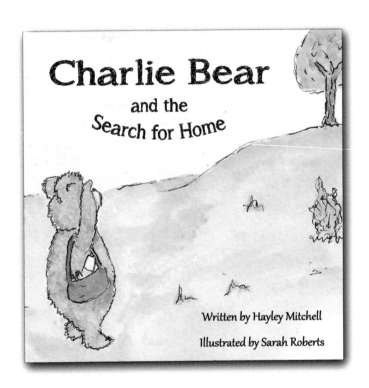

Charlie Bear
and the
Search for Home

Written by Hayley Mitchell

Illustrated by Sarah Roberts

Printed in Great Britain
by Amazon